GREEN ONIONS

Fiona L Brown

AUDACIOUS VOICES

Audacious Voices Publishing, 7 Bell Yard, London WC2A 2JR

Published in Great Britain by Audacious Voices, 2022

First paperback edition August 2022

ISBN 978-1-3999-3046-8

www.audaciousvoices.co.uk

To Phillip, of course.

And to the village around me who supply the bucket loads of coffee, gin, wine, laughs and conversations about never putting frozen potatoes in your anus.

Thank you. I love each and every one of you.

Contents

Fishing

I'd already slept with one of his colleagues, a good looking but boring guy with a big dick. It was a less than fruitful one night stand that did nothing for me, and I suspect not that much for him. Vanilla sex. No passion, no intensity, just a penis and a vagina that happened to be in the same vicinity as one another, making a physical connection with little else going on. He undressed all the way. I'm not convinced I got undressed. We were in my flat in Highbury, an expensive yet skanky place that I shared with several mice and one friend, me sleeping in what used to be the lounge but now moonlighted as a bedroom, my flatmate in the other room and the mice taking occupancy under the kitchen cupboards. Our sole communal area was the tiny kitchen in the 'penthouse' flat – which was basically the cramped top floor of a London townhouse, half of which had a sloped roof cutting off most of the standing space if you were over 5 feet tall.

His penis was a shock. What are you supposed to do when confronted by a cock that big? It was neither his nor my fault that the sex was boring. It couldn't be blamed on any particular reason other than the lack of chemistry that only becomes apparent once you've slightly sobered up away from the smoky, music filled air of the bar you've spent the last 5 hours in. Maybe it's the anticipation of sex that's sexiest. Knowing that you're taking someone home tonight and when you get to the moment, stripped bare of atmosphere and clothes, you realise it wasn't the shag you needed, it was the knowledge that you could get a shag if you wanted one. Note to self - it's *always* easier to go home and masturbate and not sleep in the wet patch.

I'd moved from Yorkshire to London for university, spending my first year living in Halls and taking part time bar work to make ends meet. I loved it. I couldn't wait to move out and had only applied to unis at least 200 miles away from my native town to ensure no-one could just 'pop' in on my new life. I'd started to feel claustrophobic where we lived. A small market town, where everyone went to school together, went out drinking together and married each other, living their days out in the same streets, breathing the same oxygen until inevitable death. I wanted, *needed*, so much more. I felt suffocated, taking in only carbon dioxide. I needed to take a breath.

Living on the Holloway Road in North London was an experience that I wasn't familiar with. Foreign men stood on every corner selling knocked off tobacco and cheap cigarettes. Wailing sirens cut through the always smoggy air. Blue lights flashed through the dusty, once cream-coloured, curtains of my tiny prison cell in halls night after night. I say prison cell but I'm been flippant. It was a small box room masquerading as a £77 per week 'student room', complete with a sink, narrow single bed, desk, and shelves, all well past their use by dates and covered in the residue of the lives that had come before me. It had a phone you had to punch the numbers into to dial and that you needed to buy a pre-paid card for. The showers were a scummy affair, with 2 at either end of the flat, which was really 6 single rooms with a shared kitchenette. Always hairy from the last user and tainted with ingrained scum from the 20 years of previous use, they did anything but make you feel clean when you got out.

Ironically the building was located behind a pub called 'The Jail', a student haunt that required wiping your feet on the way out, and a fully-fledged employer of several second-year students. When there was a bomb scare in the middle of the night because a car had been abandoned – the Londoners' version of parking – it was here that we were evacuated. This didn't make sense to me because if a car bomb was about to turn the halls of residence into a pile of rubble, I was almost certain the pub housed just underneath it would blow up too.

It's always concerning when you hear someone hammering on your flat door at 3am. The Bomb Squad vehicles were a regular sight around London streets, this being a time where terrorist attacks were still an ongoing concern. IRA dissident attacks were frequent, and although Londoners were accustomed to the threat, I'd only ever seen it on the news except for one evacuation from BHS in Leeds City Centre because of a 'suspicious package' that likely turned out to be someone's lunch. For Londoners this was commonplace but for me someone shouting 'evacuate, there's a bomb' in the middle of the night was scary. Bleary eyed, I could hear people stirring, doors opening, the raised voice of the halls manager shouting as he went from flat-to-flat telling people they might be blown to smithereens and their reaction as people started crying, shouting and laughing.

For me this was no laughing matter. Prone to anxiety since my early teens, this was my worst nightmare. I grabbed my coat and threw it over pyjama's, trying to move as quickly as possible but fighting buckling knees. My brain was willing me to move, get out, run for your fucking life, but my legs could not carry my unwilling upper body and leaden feet. Finally reaching the main door of the building after negotiating the blandly decorated and badly lit warren of corridors, I saw a calm coming over people that made me catch myself. Dean, the halls manager who was declaring imminent death by bomb to anyone who would listen, was now outside the building himself and guiding students in their favourite Mickey Mouse nightwear, presumably many had added scarves and hats for bodily protection from said bomb were it to detonate, (or maybe it was a statement of fashion and/or individuality?) into the pub. Five minutes later the bomb squad had declared the 'suspect car' as simply a badly and illegally parked car which posed no threat to anyone unless you were speeding down the 3 lanes of traffic on Parkhurst Road not expecting to see a stationery and awkwardly angled vehicle.

The story of the bomb evacuation in the dead of the night would be one that was drunkenly hammed up for effect with friends and calmly relayed to worried parents who insisted London was not the best choice of city to study in and maybe it's a decision we should re-think whilst running back to the safe, warm and boring bosom from which we came. But, no one, including me, left the halls of residence that day, or to my knowledge that year, because of the bomb scare.

I shared my halls flat with 2 guys. A straight guy from Norfolk who I would later develop a huge crush on and have sex with (twice) and a gay guy from Manchester, tall and gangly and only just becoming comfortable in his own skin. He was the one that I would share stories with of shitty sex and hideous men. He would go on to advise me not to pen that letter to our other flat mate because 'it would just be weird' and I would ignore him, write the letter anyway and things would get weird. He would also tell me that just because we had sex after dancing all night to Kandi's *'Don't think I'm Not'* I shouldn't play it on repeat because well, that's weird too and comes off as a tiny bit obsessive with a side of Psycho.

I was a small time 'Fag Hag', taking my label seriously and going to 'G-A-Y' at the Astoria, hanging out with his gay friends, and developing crushes on several (famous) gay men. (This is still a 'thing' I do. Adam Lambert and Jake Shears are on my 'list'. Harry Styles may or may not be straight/gay/either/both/everything but he's beautiful so he's on my list too). I later realised this was a safety net. Gay men don't reject you, don't leave you out, don't touch you up or try to have sex with you. They call it right when that guy you like isn't really into you and tell you honestly that he fucked you and won't be back anytime soon judging by *those* messages. When he became friends with an up-and-coming gay comedian, meeting him in trendy London hangouts and being introduced to his friends, one of whom was a very famous 1980's gay icon, he changed, and he no longer needed a Hag to his Fag. Gay men can be arseholes after all.

The rest of the flat was made up of myself, a Cypriot girl who's name we never knew because she never came out of her room in daylight, only hearing her shuffle through the darkness in the early hours, and an odd but lovely middle-class only child who was so fucked up by her father's long term affair with his secretary and her mother's subsequent admission that she had known all about it, that she spent her time watching Button Moon and Rainbow presumably to take her back to the time she was happiest and when her dad wasn't shagging someone half his age. I sometimes joined her, moving her stuffed Elmo and Cookie Monster out of the way because she was worried they'd suffocate if we sat on them, but there is nothing that will ruin your memories of childhood television programmes like watching them as an adult with another adult who is using them as regression therapy. It had never before occurred to me that Button Moon was an amalgamation of wooden spoons, Heinz baked bean tins and actual buttons. I think I may have thrown up a little bit in my mouth when I realised.

It's bizarre been thrown into a living situation with complete strangers. You quickly learn whether you're a social butterfly or an anti-social loaner. There are immediate decisions to be made based on first impressions. Are they serial killers, rapists, drug addicts or general arseholes or do they have the potential to become any of these? The latter 'arsehole' category is harder to work out than any of the former, but all have equal validity as far as I can see when living with people.

None turned out to be murderers or rapists, although one was heavily into snorting coke up his nose before he went 'Fishing' and middle-class girl had a perma-sedated (courtesy of weed) boyfriend that still lived in leafy Buckinghamshire and visited regularly. They were all curiously untidy, something which pissed me off the entire year that we lived together and something that I have never gotten over. If you live with me, you must be neat, clean and wash your fucking pubes out of the shower tray. It was the difference between the working class and the middle-class kids. The former cleaned up after themselves; the latter expected everyone else to clean up their mess. This knowledge would stand us all in good stead for adult life.

'Fishing' was the Student Union night every Wednesday. At a quid a drink it culminated in a weekly shit show in terms of drunkenness, vomit, snogging, shagging and fighting, mostly verbal, although not necessarily in that order. How the fuck anyone got up for lectures on a Thursday, or why student union nights are held mid-week remains a mystery to me even now. I tended not to drink very much, having not developed a penchant for getting hammered enough to throw up and then needing to get in those disgusting shower cubicles to wash the vomit off a body that already smelled of smoke, booze and sweat. I also stayed away from drugs. Curious you might think since they were a 'normal' part of university life. But no, they were not for me. Not before, not throughout and not after unless you count smoking flavoured tobacco from Shisha pipes in mountainous Asia which was an event I would partake in years later and was the closest I have ever come to 'doing drugs'.

Have I missed out? *Answers on a postcard please.*

The union did special nights that had an 'act' for which you needed tickets. For a fiver you could drink your weight in liquid, soft or otherwise, and watch a contortionist, a drag act or even a 'comedy' hypnotist. The hypnotist should not have been allowed to advertise himself as a hypnotist or comedic because he was not good at either the comedy or hypnotic element. He reminded me of those acts you saw on holiday with your parents in the Benidorm in the early 90's where your dad would be persuaded after too many sangrias that going up on stage and rubbing up against a woman who was not your mum with only balloons between them was a good idea. All in the name of having a fun time.

The hypnotist asked everyone in the room to clasp their hands together in front of them. A sea of reasonably intelligent people – well, this *was* a university - placed their hands together, waiting for further instruction. The idea was that if you were susceptible to hypnotism then he would be able to 'glue' your hands together and you wouldn't be able to part them. This was not my idea of fun and like fuck did I want to lose control and be brought on stage by some whack job, but I didn't want to look like an uptight cow with a rod up my arse, so I clasped my hands in front of me and wilfully ignored his words. My hands didn't become 'glued' but apparently everyone else's did. He went around the room seeking out the most extrovert people he could find, eventually settling on his human fodder in the shape of two female and two male students of whom I only knew one. A red haired, geeky boy called Liam who hung out with a 'cool' crowd he didn't appear to fit into. A crowd made up of kids who dressed in designer clothes and went home at the weekends courtesy of a credit card in their parents' names and kids from London who listened to hip hop and worked in McDonalds and Blockbusters at the weekend and who welcomed everyone into their circle. There were the white girls who loved the black boys and the black boys who loved the white girls and the middle-class coke heads who loved the other middle-class coke heads and if it sounds stereotypical it's because it was. It was nothing short of a big fat triumph for pigeon-holing and for me, it was a world far removed from what I grew up in. It was a world I loved.

It would be the native to London kids I identified most with, who I spent most of my time with and who made me feel like I finally fit in somewhere. I found solace in the music they were listening to, in the way I could grind like the girls in rap videos and no one judged me and in them taking me to underground clubs off Oxford Street that only played R ‘n’ B and where I felt most at home. The atmosphere. The music. The people. Somewhere I could just be myself. If my comfort levels on the periphery of university life came as a surprise to anyone, including me, it shouldn’t have.

For an hour the hypnotist turned them one by one into clucking chickens complete with arm movements, stomping around the small stage, the crowd lapping it up. They simulated sex with dildos and a blow-up doll, much to the amusement of the male students who jeered at the girl participants quite innocently wanking off a vibrator and playing with the toy cocks that had been hung around their necks. It was maybe half an hour in I realised that at least one of those people on stage was no more hypnotised than I was but was going along with the 'joke'. For the frivolity. The likely chance to be patted on the back the next day as having given everyone such a laugh. Everyone loved a joiner. What a sport, what a Champ. What bullshit.

The Dance

Just into my second year, I was working in Yates's in Leicester Square and heard stories about the army guys who were regular drinkers there. London having the landmarks that it does the army are aplenty. They weren't always allowed in the bar, certainly not in any big number, so they'd queue up in small groups so they could get in and congregate once they were inside hoping that the bouncers wouldn't realise what they did for a living. They also regularly shagged the bar staff who'd talk to the doormen and give them their assurances that they'd be no trouble. Yes, I did that many times. *'Come on, let them in, they're fine, they just want a drink like everyone else'. They won't cause any trouble.* Except sometimes the trouble someone brings isn't the trouble you're expecting.

I already knew Lewis through big dick guy. He knew I'd slept with big dick guy but it wasn't a contentious issue. He wanted to know if it was 'something'? Did I enjoy it? Was it great having a big cock? No, it was nothing. No, I didn't enjoy it. No, it wasn't any better with a big cock than an average size cock. He seemed placated but I don't think he'd have cared if I'd loved it and enjoyed big dick's big cock. It seemed to be pure curiosity that made him enquire. He likely knew he had always been the one I wanted; big dick guy just got there first.

Seeing him for the first time was, quite literally, one of those moments that people tell you about. It was love (or something) at first sight. I saw him across the room and bam. Mic drop. Done. Finished. End of story.

Lewis was everything. I'd noticed him a few times. I'd served him. We'd flirted. He smiled, I smiled. He made my heart race. Sometimes I swore you could see it bursting out of my chest. Like an internal drum, it hammered away whenever he was even in proximity. When I had to turn around to get a bottle from the fridge, or pour shots from the optics, I could feel myself shaking knowing that his eyes were on me. I felt self-conscious and made a massive effort when I went to work just in case he would be there. I made my black uniform trousers tight, and my dark blue work shirt as fitted as possible, knotted at the waist because no-one else wore it like that.

He was tall and broad with cornily piercing blue eyes and blonde hair – the mandatory short back and sides cut that all guys in the army were required to have and that was partly responsible for making them stand out from the rest of the customers. A large group of young men, same haircut, drinking bottled beer, wearing checked shirts with properly ironed jeans and well-polished shoes. They were easy to spot if you knew what you were looking for.

The chemistry between us was obvious to anyone with eyes. Me, him, and the other 400 people in the bar. I couldn't take my eyes off of him and I regularly caught him looking in my direction. When he was in the room my breathing was palpable, like he could constrict my airways just by being there. I'd done all the first flushes of love in my teens and had boyfriends, slept with flatmates, developed hideously inappropriate crushes but this was different. This was an intensity I couldn't explain. It was an intensity that *no one* could explain. It was this intensity that would be the beginning of the end of us. Embers like that burn strong, then fade but never entirely die. They always retain the ability to cause devastation.

I can't recall exactly how I ended up going home with him, but I did. I'd finished work behind the bar, got changed downstairs in the staff room and gone back up to have a drink with him. We talked and drank. It was the easiest and hardest conversation to have. It's easy to talk to someone when you have so much in common. When you've found the male version of yourself. It's hard to talk to someone when you believe that you'll never feel about anyone else the way you feel about them. When you've found the one that will ruin every other version of connection that you ever come across. It's hard to be able to see right from the beginning what's about to happen. It's hard to acknowledge that the beginning is actually the beginning of the end. It's impossible to try to stop yourself from getting tangled in the web. I didn't stop myself. *I had no intention of stopping myself.* I got well and truly caught in that web.

We went home to my flat in Highbury. We had sex. He was good at sex. They say that if a guy can dance then he'll be great in bed. At the weekends Yates's would have a DJ and the dance floor was always packed. Everyone danced and he was no exception. I'd watched him dance a lot and he had rhythm. I mean he could *really* move. Another thing we had in common. He felt music like I felt him. *Deeply.* Music seemed to breathe life into his soul. When he knew I was watching he'd do this kind of grind against the bar, slowly and methodically, in complete harmony with whatever music was playing. He was basically showing me what fucking him was like. Slow. Deep. Heated. Rhythmic. He knew it turned me on, so he did it more. Sometimes I asked him to do it. Sometimes he obliged and sometimes he didn't. That would come to be our rhythm. *C'est la vie.*

The sex was great. *It would be that way until the last time*. The sex was insane. When you can't stop looking into someone's eyes it always is. Undressed, dressed, I couldn't not look at him. His entire being pulled me towards him. I could sense when he was there. I could sense when he wasn't there. You could turn me around with my back to the crowd of the bar and I could tell you if he was in the room or not. The pull was that strong. That sort of connection can't be paused. There's no room for rewind or fast forward. You can't erase it. You can't deny it. You can only press play and let it be. Pure magnetism. Pure chemistry. *Pure disaster.*

I knew I'd see him at work. I wasn't sure if it would be awkward or not. The next time he came in the bar he caught my eye and winked at me. He would do that every time until he didn't.

When he winked I smiled. He smiled back. Something about his eyes made my heart pound. Being around him put me on edge. I worked the long bar, serving hundreds of people on any given night, and even through those crowds I could feel his constant gaze laying heavy on me. I could sense him all the time. He was the only person I'd ever met in my life that I had a sixth sense for. He was the only person I'd ever met in my life that seemed to be able to see right into me. We shunted each other. *Back. Forth. Push. Pull. Together. Apart. Attract. Repel.* It, *He*, gave me chills. *Good and bad.*

He told me he was working the next night at a place where they got ready for ceremonial duties. They weren't allowed out, but I could come down there if I wanted. I asked if it was *really okay* for me to be there? It would be fine he said. I took his word. It was thrilling in every sense. Who doesn't want to be invited into someone's life like that? I was about to get an intimate snapshot of what he did for a living, at a place where civilians weren't supposed to be or see. He was going out on a limb for me to be there. He'd have to sneak me in. And out. I'd have to be surreptitious. He could’ve asked me to make myself invisible and I would have made it happen. I’d already do anything for him. He had me. *All of me.*

It was only a short walk from my work, and they were based there twice every week. After a few times staying there I’d come across many a woman thrown out of the gates at the crack of dawn before an officer spotted her. I always recognised the look because I’d been there too, sometimes with my knickers screwed up in my bag, last night’s lipstick staining my lips and shivering in the early London air, wishing I’d taken a coat the night before so I could complete the ‘Walk of Shame’ amongst the black cabbies and street cleaners with at least the tiny amount of dignity that covering any bare limbs would provide.

That first time there were a group of us that ended up there. Four girls, one of which was my flatmate who also worked at Yates's with me and who wasn't interested in any of the guys and was just along for the ride and moral support on account of my ridiculous mix of nerves and excitement that threatened to get the better of me and mean I might not turn up. The other two were acquaintances who I'd seen hanging around with the guys in the bar, who I would come to know, grow friendly with, and one I would even share a flat with whilst we were both still fucking our respective army guys. *Three out of four of us would end up marrying military men, but that's another story.*

We sat in some communal area where there was a TV and beers, chatting and watching some action film. I didn't care much for the film. It's not what I was there for, and I was grateful when we eventually went our separate ways, my flatmate making her way home and the other two disappearing somewhere that I didn't care. I went with Lewis upstairs to where they slept and we pitched ourselves on an old black leather couch that was cracked and soft and had seen better days and no doubt, plenty of action.

It felt weird being in a room full of empty beds that would soon play host to sleeping men, about to represent Queen and Country. It was how I imagined a private school would be laid out, only grottier with smaller beds. No privacy, worn out carpets, uniforms hanging ready for the next day and beds made with precision. Everything was compartmentalised. Such was life in the army.

We knew we shared a love of music. A notion that only added to the passion when you realise someone is into the same thing as you. He loved Motown and old R'n'B – the real Rhythm and Blues stuff where the guys played harmonica and sang about heartache while swigging bourbon on a rickety, wooden porch. Some of the music I didn't know much about, but he would initiate me into a whole new world. I'd been brought up with music loving parents, my father having the entire Motown collection on pristine vinyl in alphabetical order. I loved mainstream R'n'B – what would later become known as 'Old Skool' and would get on board with anything that he loved because surely then *he would love me?*

The area where we were sitting was exposed and at one end of the dorm where they slept, directly next to the door that led to the toilets and shower rooms. If you needed the toilet there were no separate women's facilities this being a male only regiment - so you had to risk quickly running into a manky cubicle hoping you didn't bump into any of the other guys and weeing as quickly as possible before making a dash back to wherever you'd been holed up, hoping you hadn't been seen in whatever various state of undress you were in.

We sat on the sofa close enough to share earphones to his CD Walkman, our legs consciously touching. Why did it feel like this when we'd already had sex? If there was an icebreaker it was surely sleeping with someone yet the heat still rose from my skin and my head was still dizzy being this close to him, feeling him breathe, watching his body. I studied everything about him. What he was wearing. *A black top and dark blue adidas bottoms. Odd socks*. The colour of his eyes. *Crystal blue.* The way his hair was parted. *To the left.*

He put on Boyz II Men, a group I knew and loved. He always seemed to be moved by music. I felt the same. But as the songs were playing and we were listening, pretending that that's all we were doing but really working ourselves up to what was coming next, what we were about to do, he told me how they'd played *'It's so hard to say goodbye to Yesterday'* at his friend's funeral. I didn't know what to say. *Great choice for a funeral song?* It felt like a lot to tell me. Something so personal. So meaningful. It weighed heavy on me, on him. Where do you go from that?

He told me outright, as we sat with an earphone each, that we weren't having sex. I said okay because I knew we were. I have a tendency to get something when I want it and I wanted him. I also knew once you'd had sex with someone once it was much easier to go down that path again. And also, *why else was I there?* Why had he invited me? Bullshit, of course we were having sex.

Maybe it was because *'End of The Road'* was playing that he gave in because it's definitely a song that made us both feel 'something', but suddenly we were kissing and he was hard and the CD was spinning in the Walkman on the floor and we were in a sleeping bag but I'm not sure how and he was naked, I was undressed from the waist down and then he was in me and I've never wanted anyone more than I did at that moment. He stopped, but only because a guy walked past on his way to the showers because it's almost 4am and we've been up all night listening to

Water Runs Dry and *One Sweet Day* and the funeral song on repeat. The guy laughed and apologised but it's not awkward because it's clear that this stuff happened all the time. Lewis laughed too and carried on, his head buried into my neck. I watched his tattooed body moving. *Beautiful*. He finished, I didn't. He had to get me out of there before anyone saw me. I took my underwear out of the boots I'd taken earlier – it had seemed the best place to shove them for safe keeping – and got dressed in the modesty of the sleeping bag. He ushered me downstairs, avoiding his superiors who wouldn't be impressed that he'd been up all night, or that he'd been fucking some girl when he was about to be paraded out in front of all the tourists and shoved me out onto the still dark streets of London where I'd take the night bus back to Highbury and on the way a group of drunken men would walk past me and one would grab me between the legs. I would go home and cry because of the assault. And because he left me to fend for myself. And because he was protecting fucking Queen and Country but didn't seem to give a shit about protecting me. And because I knew it wasn't his job to protect me. And because I knew I should've protected myself. *And because I knew this wouldn't be the last time that I'd feel this way.*

I don't know how long it was before I saw him again. Probably only days that turned into an eternity in my head. I was already obsessed. With Lewis, with the music, with his body and his tattoos and his eyes and his hair and his accent. I couldn't think straight and could only process thoughts about him. I missed lectures because I couldn't share the brain space with the space I needed for him.

He came first, always. Thoughts of him would consume me for a very long time, well after the last time I saw him and long into my first marriage which would eventually break down not *because* of him but *because it always should have been him.*

The sex was as intense as we were and often seemed to depend on his musical mood which could dictate his entire 'being' at any given moment. When I was working behind the bar and he was drinking with his friends he would give me that wink across the room. I felt his eyes on me wherever I moved. He had this ability to suddenly appear at the front of the 3-person deep queue that ran the length of the interior on weekend evenings. I served him first always, to the disdain of disgruntled pissheads who'd already been waiting 10 minutes to get served, but it was common knowledge amongst the staff that we were a ‘thing’ and it was to be expected that he would get preferential treatment. Everyone else could’ve been dying of thirst and I’d have let them. *So unprofessional.*

The advice to always put your own oxygen mask on first before you helped anyone else would be lost on me when it came to him. I gave him all the oxygen he needed and suffocated myself in the process.

He played guitar well, softly working the strings, head down, mostly silent in his thoughts and sometimes humming along to the music he was making. He came across as brooding, but my feeling was that he was the deepest soul I’d ever met. Sometimes I wanted to reach inside him and set him free from his thoughts. He seemed like he always wanted to distance himself from the moment in favour of losing himself in the music. I’m not sure how present he ever was in a moment that involved or didn't involve music. If there was music it would take over him, if there was no music, he'd be playing it silently in his head detached from any reality. *That was his obsession.*

I enjoyed listening to him. I could become quite mesmerised watching him. I never wanted to interrupt him so I didn't speak or sing or hum. There was no point anyway. I could never compete with the love affair he had with the rhythm. I allowed the moment to pass until his spiritual self was once again part of his physical self. I wondered if he knew how it felt to be mesmerised by *someone* and not *something*. To not have to hear it or play it or make it but to be able to feel it. *To feel me*. Would he ever be able to acknowledge it? Would he ever be able to acknowledge me in the same way I acknowledged him? I wondered if he knew what he was missing. *I wondered if he was missing anything at all.*

I knew all along that he had a girlfriend in his hometown of Brighton. It had come up quite early on as a topic of conversation. Definitely before we slept together for the first time. I knew that she was my namesake. I thought that it was sickeningly convenient. I didn't know if there were in love. *I* loved him. I think it had been a high school thing. They knew each other's families. When he left for the army they'd simply stayed 'boyfriend and girlfriend'. He told me that they were too young to be serious. *I* was serious. He told me she could never find out about us. Us. *What was 'us'?* I agreed. I wanted nothing but him. I had no feelings towards her although the thought of him going home some weekend's and having sex with her was something I would never be able to deal with so I didn't think about it. I had no thoughts about it and I was thankful for the gruelling army schedule that kept him from his family, and her, most of the time.

Our birthdays were days apart. Both Librans, falling easily and hard in and out of love, gathering obsessions, feeling things too deeply, not deeply enough, feeling uncontrollable passion and uncontrollable anger. Neither of us capable of making any firm decisions without ensuing angst. We would eventually burn out because of all of these. This, and the very intense pain we would cause each other. In Psychology there is a known condition relating to overwhelming obsession. It says that if your obsession overly consumes you then other things in your life risk losing any value and you become capable of tolerating the demise of everything else around you but for the obsession. *A concept that was becoming increasingly familiar for me.*

I didn't know what to get him for his birthday, but I wanted to get him *something*. I figured music was the way to go but it had to be personal. My brother had this clever software that could find any song that you wanted and then burn it onto a CD. I compiled the following list: *These Arms of Mine (Otis Redding), Cry to Me (Solomon Burke), Mercy Mercy Me (Marvin Gaye), In the Still of the Night (The Five Satins), Let's stay together (Al Green), Love Man (Otis Redding), Green Onions (Booker T and the MGs), End of The Road (Boyz II Men), If you don't know me by now (Harold Melvin and The Blue Notes), I'll make love to you (Boyz II Men), Sittin' on The Dock of The Bay (Otis Redding) Some kind of Wonderful (The*

Drifters), How can you mend a broken heart (Al Green), Me and Mrs Jones (Billy Paul). My brother, in his early teens at the time and a tech whizz, placed tiny pictures of the albums that he'd taken the music from on the CD, put it in a clear case and sent it to me in the post.

The night of his birthday we were out celebrating in Yates's. Despite me working there many hours of the week I liked spending my spare time there. It was comfortable and easy and there was always a chance Lewis might be there. When Yates's closed at 1am, we walked to Cheers Bar on Regent Street because it stayed open for another 2 hours. It was a bar that based itself on the 1980's TV programme *'Cheers'* and that was popular with tourists, squaddies and their groupies alike. You would often bump into someone you knew from 'the crowd' in there at the weekend. Just like it said in the opening credits of the show, it was the bar *where everybody knows your name*. We danced and drank cocktails called 'Green Witch' and 'Love Buzz'. We watched each other. He never kissed me in bars. He never held my hand. He sometimes danced near me, sometimes he was even close enough that we accidentally brushed limb against limb. I liked dancing near him. *This was the way we danced for a long time.*

I told him I had something for his birthday. He said I shouldn't buy him anything. I hadn't so that was fine. I handed him the CD as we tried to find a cab to take us back to my place which was now in Hammersmith with a bigger kitchen with a dining room table and no mice but a landlord who thought he could let himself in whenever he wanted. He thanked me and asked me what was on there.

I didn't tell him, said it was a surprise and to listen to it. He said he'd play it when he was back at the barracks. We dropped off his best friend, who hated me, first and then chatted and laughed all the way back to mine.

Birthday sex is always good. Who doesn't want to get laid on their birthday? It was double whammy because it was my birthday in a few days too. We kissed and he undressed. He put me on all fours on the bed, my huge dressing table mirror just off to our front right. I had a clear view as he took me from behind, his hands holding my hips, the tense muscles of his tattooed arms. I didn't like watching myself, but I liked watching him and he liked it. We'd already tried everything in bed and this night was no different so when he asked me where I wanted 'it' I told him he could put 'it' anywhere, which he did. When I later went down on him, he laid still for a while, me to sucking him until he was bored then he told me I could stop. I laid next to him on the bed and he lit a cigarette.

I liked watching him smoke. He had a James Dean feel about him. He always smoked after sex. He smoked a lot. I didn't smoke and I doubt he would've liked it if I had. He slid his jeans on, opened the tall sash window and lit another cigarette blowing the smoke out of the window. We were talking about music. A conversation he would willingly have any time of day or night. I'm not sure why but he leant against the door jamb and started humming along to Al Green's 'Let's stay together', *'Whyyyyy ....mmmmm ..... why people break-up, mmmmm.... turn around .... make-up ...mmmmm... .... You'd never do that to me ......'*

I let the words wash over me as he sang. He was singing it to me, in *my* bedroom, in *my* flat. He had a nice voice, none of his Brighton accent coming through the melody. Maybe that was his way of saying what he wanted to say to me. I was glad I'd included the song on his CD. He would realise that once he listened to it. Music seemed to come easier to him than words. Sometimes I thought he could only feel through music, living vicariously through the words of musicians who'd come long before him. I took a mental picture of that moment to retain for when we would no longer be doing this. Whatever *'this'* was. Of course, I already knew this wasn't permanent. *He* wasn't permanent. His type of soul couldn't give that to anyone. He wasn't meant to belong to just one person. *And I was already certain he didn't want to belong to me.*

Birthday Girl

He wasn't sure he could make it. It would be last minute if he could. When he turned up in the bar it felt good. He didn't bring a card or gift, but he brought himself. That's what mattered. His best friend was by his side. *In his shadow*. The Robin to his Batman, they were together always. I'm not sure I'd ever seen one without the other, but it seemed to me that the friend needed him more than the other way around. They had joined up together, but he had delayed his friend. He told me that his friend could have joined whenever he wanted but waited 2 years for him because of some issue with the medical paperwork. It took until they were both 18 to join, putting them 2 years behind a lot of the guys who joined up at 16.

The friend didn't usually pay any of the squaddie groupies any attention and I don't recall seeing him with a girlfriend. He was one of the boys and wasn't interested in mingling with the girls who hung around them – particularly the one who hung around his best friend. But tonight he made a point of speaking to me. It was one of the very few times we conversed. He wanted to tell me something. He wanted to tell me that Lewis had listened to the CD I made and that the songs were good choices. He told me that I must know him *really* well to be able to choose all those songs for him. That they were his type of music. I could tell the friend was surprised as he told me this – likely as surprised as I was by the fact that he was bothering to speak to me and tell me this at all. I didn't understand why he was surprised that I knew Lewis so well. *That's just what happens when someone already inhabits your soul.*

We danced and drank. We went back to the barracks. To get a girl in there it was basically potluck who was in the Guard room which was like their reception area that you had to walk through to get in. Tonight we were lucky. This guy knew us and didn't mind me coming in but I had to have a photo taken and give my details for a visitor pass to make it 'official'. I'd been to the barracks before and they'd never said that but maybe for regular visitors it was easier that way. Or maybe they wanted to make it as awkward as possible. Or maybe they took all your details to run a background check on you? It would make sense when you're going onto military property that they don't want to let any old crackpot in. *Stranger things have happened.* It occurred to me that his girlfriend may also have had her photo taken for a pass. I wondered where she was in the system in relation to me. Was it first name alphabetical in which case we would be next to each other and would allow them the easiest game of compare and contrast ever. If it was surname alphabetical then who knew. If it was in date order she would almost certainly be above me. I stood still while they took my picture, suddenly ridiculously self-conscious of my face, my body, my clothes and the fact that I was even here with him, understanding that they would likely know far more about our relationship – for want of a better word – than I did. Or maybe he didn't tell them anything. He obviously wasn't embarrassed to be with me if he was bringing me here regularly. Was this a good sign?

Despite them being grown men they messed about with the picture on the computer making me moustachioed and adding glasses, laughing at themselves. And probably me. I laughed because I didn't want it to appear like I cared, but it made me feel small and stupid, the brunt of their joke. Lewis didn't say anything to stop them, but he didn't join in laughing either. I got the impression he thought it was childish too. He was deeper than this. Better than this. I wondered how many girls with drawn on beards there were in the system.

We went up to his sleeping area. They slept 6, maybe 8, to a room in a dorm style. Single beds with cupboards stood between them giving only a sense of, but no actual, privacy.

The room had a couple of guys in and he somehow got rid of them. Army guys were good to each other like that. If one was on a promise of getting laid then they'd make themselves scarce. We were alone. I was relieved. I never relaxed in the barracks. It wasn't exactly female friendly. No female staff. No female toilets. Half-naked guys everywhere, walking to the showers after a long day at work, getting ready to go to work on an early shift. I wondered if it made them feel awkward too. Some random woman in the place where they lived, slept, showered, got dressed. Maybe they hated it. It was an intrusion of their privacy. But I still felt like I was being watched all the time. That I was being judged. That all the guys were in on a secret that I wasn't. That I was on the guest list for the party but when I arrived someone stopped me from getting in.

He played the CD. He told me he really liked it. That the other guys really liked it too. *He must've told them that I got it for him.* He said I had good taste. *That was true*. He came alive listening to these songs. He talked to me about everything he knew about the singers, the songs, the melodies, the notes, the words. It brought him to life. I told him I didn't know '*Green Onions*' existed until I met him although I thought I remembered hearing it on a TV advert once. That was the most valuable, and only, gift he would ever give to me. *Green Onions.* And all the other music that I'd never experience in the way I experienced it with him. The fact that so many songs I loved had an original version from years before that I knew nothing about but that he could instantly tell me. Even the funeral song by Boyz II Men had really been cover of an old G.C Cameron hit from the

1970's. This was the stuff he gave to me. It was something no one else would ever give me, *could* ever give me. When we finally reached Booker T and the MG's we sat in silence listening and taking it in. Whenever I heard it in the future it would remind me of him. *Always.*

He picked up his guitar and started to play. He was a genuine talent. I thought one day I'd see his name in lights. He had his shirt off. I touched his back, balancing on the tiny bed not wanting to disturb him but needing to feel him. I felt music too. I found it powerful. But to him the power overtook everything else. I wish I could've felt what was running through his veins like he did. Experience that level of euphoria from something so simple. I wanted to understand whatever it was that was so powerful to him that the human beside him could pale into insignificance. To understand whatever it was that stopped him responding to my touch.

We kissed but I was powerless compared to his guitar and it turned into nothing. I kissed his chest, his stomach. Unzipped his jeans. Went down on him. He told me he had to be up at 5am. 4 hours from now. He slept on his side. I didn't sleep. *Happy birthday to me.*

Family Day

Every year they had to go on a summer training exercise to Scotland. Each year the trip would culminate in 'Family Day' where friends, family and *girlfriends* would go and chat, socialise and mingle with the other families. There was some kind of display. I imagined it would be a lovely day talking about how proud you were of your son/husband/boyfriend. *Look how handsome he looks in his uniform. We're so proud of him. He works so hard. Look how shiny they get their boots. They must be so warm in all those layers. I wish we saw him more often.* I didn't get an invite to Family Day.

The local pub had rooms for rent for £40 a night and served food. National Exprcss coaches ran a service from London that stopped right outside there. I was struggling to afford rent but I could juggle things around to make it work. I booked a room in the pub and a coach ticket. I wasn't sure how it'd worked out like this, but I would be there the night before family day.

The village nearby was a small affair that had stood still since the 1980's. It felt like an incestuous place. One of those villages where everyone knows everyone else. Where Sarah married her mum's best friend's nephew and John's uncle happens to be Sarah's second cousin. It didn't feel dissimilar to the place I'd escaped from, and I really didn't want to stay. Crossing the road to the local shop I felt conspicuous. *All eyes on me.* I was a stranger, a foreigner in their land and it was obvious. It occurred to me in the time I'd spent in London not once had I felt like that. In London I belonged. In London no one cared who I was, or who my aunt was, or who I went to school with. In London I was a stranger, a foreigner, but I was a welcome one.

He knew I was going. I didn't just turn up. *That would be lunacy.* He seemed to have no major objections. I assumed that when you're going away with all men for weeks at a time, your long-term shag turning up is probably not the worst thing in the world.

When I arrived I sent him a message to let him know I was there. Lewis came to meet me. We had a drink in the bar and went to the room. I got changed in the tiny en-suite bathroom, brushing my teeth, touching up my make-up, getting myself ready for him. He was shirtless when I came out of there. We sat on the bed chatting about how it'd been going. We talked about life.

Me - How was work?

Lewis – Fine. Same old.

Lewis – How's uni?

Me – Fine. Exams are finished. Looking for some temp work to make extra money.

Lewis - The room isn't too bad for the money is it.

Me – No, it's fine.

Sometimes what we were doing felt normal. In the privacy of just us, behind these closed doors, we were just two human beings who felt something for each other, who liked each other, who had similar interests, who found it easy to be in each other's company. It felt like we were the most normal people on earth. My mind would continually fast forward to a time when this was 'our' normal. When we booked a hotel *together.* When we travelled there *together.* And when he wasn't making sure I knew that he couldn't be seen with me anywhere in the village. *I was imagining a time when I was the one going to 'Family Day'.*

Had I had the knowledge then that somewhere along the line we would end up standing in a room full of people not even able to acknowledge the other's presence I might have told you it was a crazy thought. How could we ever not be friends? How could we have experienced each other in the way we had and now pretend we don't even know each other. *How could we do so much harm?*

He, only half-jokingly, told me not to mark him because he didn't want his girlfriend to see tomorrow. It might have been an odd thing for him to say because I didn't recall marking him before, it wasn't really my style, but it was Family Day and she would be there and maybe he was stressed, worried that he'd give the game away. We'd been doing this for so long in London, away from prying eyes and in the company of people who would always cover for us if the situation ever arose, that bringing it so close to the danger zone was probably stupid. But love and sex and passion and want and need are strong pulls towards doing stupid things. Things you never imagined yourself to be capable of. Did I envisage being the 'other woman' to the man I was deeply in love with? Not really. Did I want to share his mind, his body, his soul with someone else, someone who I was certain didn't get him like I did, hadn't connected with him like I had? Of course I didn't. This was just the reality of it. A reality that turned my stomach. Vomit stung the back of my throat. I swallowed it back down. I knew the deal. I could hardly start kicking up a fuss now. I could hardly ask how the fuck he could be here doing this and be able to face either of us. I could hardly ask how the fuck he could face himself in the mirror knowing what he was doing. I could hardly ask him any of those things when facing myself in the mirror was becoming increasingly difficult. Was there ever a good enough reason to be doing this? Could you ever be so blindly in love that this was okay? How long do you allow it to go on like this? Accepting the status quo of something so fucked up was, in every sense, permitting it. But how did you stop it? Could you stop it? Should you only stop something if you're inclined to, and it you don't have the inclination are you still guilty?

The short answer was that I couldn't stop it and I didn't care.

He laid on the bed and I straddled him, and, only half-jokingly, sucked on his neck. Shit. Had I given him a love bite? Nope, no marks. *Better luck next time*. I remember one of the girls Izzy, who I'd got to know as part of the 'squaddie' crowd, telling me that when she was fucking her guy she liked to pull hard on the crucifix around his neck that had been a gift from his girlfriend. She said he always worried that she'd snap it and that he'd have to lie about it the next time he went home or that she'd leave such deep lines on his neck that the girlfriend would realise what was going on. With the crucifix in her hand she literally had the power. At that moment in time, a moment where he was inside her and she was riding him, yanking at the chain, hoping it would leave red marks on his skin and knowing that he didn't really *care* whether it left a mark or not, because if he *truly* cared he wouldn't be fucking her and taking the risk, she held all the cards. *What a nice place to be.*

Izzy was the perfect woman. She was tall, leggy, with long blonde hair and blue eyes. Attractive, funny, super confident and bright. The guys liked her, although Lewis wasn't a fan, nor she of him. I thought that was weird sometimes. It crossed my mind that they might have had a frisson at some point. They'd known each other longer because she was part of the group before me, so it was feasible. At some point I'm sure I asked him but I'm not sure I ever asked her. He told me no. Her answer may have been different. Gut instinct told me they hadn't but maybe one of them had wanted to and that maybe lust had turned into dislike. *There's a thin line between love and hate.*

She was the girl with the guy friends and the girl friends. Popular. Everyone loved Izzy. I grew to love Izzy. I ended up living with her. She was a final year Physiotherapy student close to graduation. She cooked herself steak in red wine sauce in the evenings and bought beautiful long winter coats in white that I was jealous of. I didn't eat meat and the coat wouldn't have suited me. I was simply jealous of the freedom she had to do both. At this point she seemed so sophisticated. I liked her and loathed her all at the same time. I think she looked down on me, with no malice, but she was very definitely middle class, and I was still very definitely working class. I was Northern, she was Southern. From the Home Counties no less. She was what I might have considered back then to be 'posh'.

My adulthood was moving on because, despite all the differences, we built a solid friendship. We shared a love of our cheating guys, of R'n'B, of dancing, of dressing up at the weekend, of enjoying life. We smashed it on the dance floor together and we drank cocktails until we couldn't drink anymore. We slept with other people, we kissed some of the same people although never at the same time. We snuck into the barracks together, we went to a huge Ministry of Sound Halloween party dressed as sexy zombie's together and I crashed on the floor of her bedroom so when we woke up in the morning we could relive all the details together over strong coffee and smudged mascara. She even came home with me for a family party and stayed at my parent's house. I hated it when our friendship dissolved into nothing. I hated it when I heard her talking about me to our other flatmate because they thought I was at work when I was really slumped behind my bedroom door silently sobbing because my life was crumbling around me. I hated that they blamed me for being a shit friend, for earning less than they did, for wanting the life that they had but that I couldn't seem to achieve. *But most of all I ended up hating myself.*

In the bland room, above an ancient pub on a high street that had seen better days, we had good, no *great*, sex. We kissed and we touched and we orgasmed and we had hot, dirty, passionate sex for as long as we could.

I couldn't tell you what it was that made it great that night. The false sense of normality, the privacy or possibly the need to prove to him that it was me he needed. That no one could fuck him like I could fuck him. That it was me that should be at Family Day. That it should be me proudly watching him parade around in his full ceremonial uniform. Me stood with his parents with tears in our eyes. Instead, it would be her doing those things. Instead the only thing I was left with were the tears in my own eyes.

He left early. It made a change that it was him scurrying out of somewhere before sunrise rather than me. I told him I hoped 'Family Day' went well. He never kissed me goodbye. The morning after was always so alien to the night before. The man that joined me in the evenings was not the same one that left me in the mornings. The man who kissed me readily in private never did in public. The man who shared so much with me after the sunset but kept so much from me before sunrise. The man who had so much of me, who held my heart and soul in his hands, who willingly claimed them as his own and who I willingly gave them to never willingly handed me anything.

Here is a list of things that I wish I'd told him that night:

1. I loved him.
2. This had to stop.
3. He had scratch marks on his back.

Life often works in mysterious ways and in this small pub with rooms above it in this sleepy, strange village is where I would spend a night the following year. It would be because 'Family Day' was happening again. I would book the National Express coach service from London and I would arrive the night before. That time I would wait hours to be met at the pub. I would call and call but there was no answer. When he finally arrived we went to Tesco, a mundane but exciting task when you aren't normally seen in public with the man you're sleeping with. We had chemistry even in the supermarket and I enjoyed the normality with him, imagining a future where we would do the weekly shopping arguing about the flavour crisps we bought or whether to get white or brown bread. We bought snacks for the room. We split the cost. As we drove back I saw a deer running through the fields. I told him that I'd never seen a deer in real life, not in the wild anyway. He was shocked and told me there were loads around here and that he saw them all the time. I thought he was lucky to see that with his own eyes so regularly. I never took those things for granted.

In the room we ate crisps, drank coke, mine diet, went to bed and had sex. Average sex that we both fell asleep in the middle of. He had a huge tattoo across his back that I traced with my finger. He fell asleep and slept next to me all night. When he went to work the next day we said our goodbyes. Once again I was not going to ‘Family Day’ but his mum and his son would be.

My Lass

There were a handful of places in London that you were guaranteed to find army guys if you so desired. Yates's in Leicester Square, Long Island Iced Tea Bar on St Martins Lane and Cheers Bar on Regent Street. On the odd occasion you'd also find them in The Rock Garden or Roadhouse in Covent Garden. Tonight we were in Long Island and it was full of them. Except Lewis. He was working, doing '*Duty*' but I was going back there later. I was with the group of girls who I'd met through them. Only one couple were in a bone fide, genuine relationship. They were getting married and watched as the rest of us flailed around trying to make something out of nothing, understanding that they had everything. The husband to be sometimes acted as a go between telling us if he thought the guys were serious, weren't interested, general arseholes, fucking other girls or good blokes. Most of the time, I'm certain, he kept their secrets close to his chest.

He introduced us to a new guy. Dark haired, good looking and tattooed. Apparently he had transferred from another barracks. It's quite normal in the army so I didn't ask why. He was having a hard time with the other guys and husband to be had taken him under his wing. We chatted, he seemed nice enough, if I hadn't been involved with someone he worked with *I might* have considered it.

As we chatted it became apparent he wasn't a fan of Lewis, or really any of the guys I knew. I'm not sure why but it seemed they weren't being exactly friendly. When I later talked to Lewis about it, it was clear the feeling was mutual. No one liked the new guy, he was a knob, he fancied himself, he didn't fit in. They'd heard things about him. *He was an outsider*. I quite liked outsiders because I felt like an outsider too.

We danced until the early hours. I liked places with an R'n'B and Hip-Hop vibe – the stuff you could *really* dance to. Nelly and Kelly were having a *Dilemma*, Justin Timberlake was rocking your body, Eve was blowing everyone's mind, Fatman Scoop was telling everyone to *Be Faithful* and Truth Hurts with Rakim's latest song was appropriately called '*Addictive*'. They were playing the soundtrack to our lives.

Downstairs, in that small, dark, hot club, we danced until our hair stuck to our faces and our make-up was barely existent. The guys kissed the girls and got upset if the girl they were with got attention from another man. The girls danced like their lives depended on it. Dance like a queen. Keep it classy but be sexy. Suggestive. It was a way of enticing your guy. *Come see what I've got. Look, this is all for you. Keep your eyes on me, no one else.* Tonight I didn't have Lewis's eyes on me, but I certainly had all the other guys watching, ready to tell him about any flirtations, making sure *his girl* was faithful. Loyal. Making sure no one else got what he already had. He needn't have worried. These days I didn't have any thoughts that weren't about him. As far as I was concerned, I belonged entirely to him and I was always happy when they reported back to him that his girl was a good girl.

I was staying at the place they did duty that night. I went there knowing I wouldn't get any sleep and that I'd be on the night bus home by 5am. When I got there he had got the only bed that had any privacy, around a tight corner and away from the rest of the dorm style set up. Every guy tried to get that bed when they were on duty and wanted to invite a girl back. He must have been lucky. Maybe he won a bet. *Did they draw straws to see who could have a semi-private shag at night?* A tall sash window to the left gave us a view down onto the busy London streets that even in the dark were always lit up because of the sheer volume of orange streetlights lining the pavements only yards apart. When you watched closely you were given an insight into the journey home habits of young Londoners. There were the kebab eaters, the touching each other up in a doorway couple, the vomiting girls, the fighting boys and the happy, giggling groups staggering back to their overly expensive flat shares. I liked been up here watching them. I felt safe. *Down there you were exposed to everything.*

The beds were barely even single size. More like camp beds. He had his guitar. I guess it passed the time they were there and not able to go out anywhere, waiting for their girl, *any girl,* to arrive. He sat opposite on another bed, polishing his boots for work the next day. They called it 'bulling your boots'. It meant getting them to shine to the point where you could pretty much see your face in them. They needed to look like glass. A self-made mirror that they could see themselves in. I doubted any of them ever really saw themselves.

He took the boot shining seriously. I suppose it was serious. I'm certain they were inspected before parade and reprimanded if they didn't meet the strict requirements. It took a long time and we talked as he polished and shined, polished and buffed, polished and shined over and over. He took pride in his work and he wasn't the type that would take kindly to a bollocking so he kept going until his hand hurt. He asked me to throw him his lighter that was next to me. They used it as some kind of method to heat the boot so that the wax melted into the leather. I picked it up and gently threw it over to him not considering the disaster that this could have caused and missing his boots by a millimetre. His face, just for a split second, was sheer terror. I wasn't sure how angry he might have been had I scratched those boots. I didn't want to find out. *I would hate it if he was mad at me, even for a stupid mistake.* I still don't know why I threw it rather than stand up and walk over, but I think it was so I didn't draw attention to myself. It was always a weird situation to be there however many times you'd been or however familiar with the other guys you were, and I hated that feeling of conspicuousness that I always got when I was there alone, just waiting to have sex. *Like an unpaid hooker.*

We chatted about rules, uniform and work the next day until he was happy the boots were shiny enough and he placed them next to the bed. He put music on and we listened for a while. I loved singing along to these songs at home, I'd sing my heart out, feeling every note, every word, but not in front of him. How could I? Music was so special to him, I didn't want to ruin it. He shouldn't be made to hear or remember my voice over theirs. Harold Melvin and The Blue Notes softly sang '*if you don't know me by now, you will never ever, ever know me…*' it was a song he really liked, and one I had come to know and love. I could recite every word. I wondered if it had particular meaning to him, like the funeral song. I wondered if he played it because the words meant something. I wondered if he wanted me to hear these particular words. Was he telling me that I didn't know him well enough? Or maybe that I'd never really know him. Or was he scared I already knew him too well? *Double bluff.*

I was laid on my side on the bed fully dressed. I had on black trousers that showed my belly button and a silky wrap top that tied at one side of the waist. I was a slim size 12 but I felt huge next to the girls I knew. They were tall and very slim, small and very slim, or average height and very slim. In reality of course so was I, but if your stumpy size 12 legs jutted up against your flatmate's size 8 'up to her armpits' legs on the tube, there was a noticeable difference. It wasn't something that made me super self-conscious, I liked my body, and I knew how to use it when I needed to, but I definitely felt like the 'biggest' in the group. I was the girl who had to really think about what to wear tonight. I wasn't the 'pull anything out of the wardrobe and make it work' girl that's for sure. That was Izzy's domain.

He got undressed. I don't recall whether we kissed or not. He turned me over onto my front, face down, and he slid my hipster trousers down, then my underwear, then he laid on top of me and took me like that. I liked the feeling of him covering me up like that, protecting me from the outside world. He had his arms around me, and even though I couldn't see his face I knew he was into it. It felt good. We fell asleep and I woke just before 5am to get dressed and get out. My fumbling to get my clothes on woke him up and he tiredly asked me what time it was. When I told him he jumped out of bed, berating me for not getting him up sooner because he had to get me out and get ready for work. He pulled a towel around his waist, walked me downstairs and sent me out into the cool London streets. *Some things never change.*

I don't really recall the exact timing but someone told me they broke up. Eventually *he* told me they broke up. There was no girlfriend from home anymore. Lewis told me it didn't mean anything. He told me it wasn't because of me. My mind raced though. Why, how, when. Of course, I didn't ask any of those things. I felt like it wasn't my business. I had no idea this was about to happen. I hadn't thought about it in a long time. It was one of those pieces of information that you had to repress. I would ask him about it at some point in the future and he would tell me they'd long since drifted apart. They barely saw each other. She wasn't into it anymore. He wasn't into it anymore. They'd just grown apart. I wondered if you had to grow together in the first place to be able to ever grow apart. Could it ever work when one of you was deep in it and the other was only dipping their toe in? It wasn't lost on me that he had only been dipping his toe in with both of us for a long time.

They worked not far from a large park. Popular with students, locals and tourists as a green haven in town, somewhere to meet, to exercise, I liked venturing there whenever I could. It was close to where he would be. *It made me feel close to him*. I was hunting for the girls. We'd arranged a picnic and drinks. As I was walking through the park my mobile phone rang. It was Lewis. He asked where I was, and I told him I was walking through the park to meet the girls. He told me he could see me. I laughed. Of course he couldn't see me. He said I had a blue bag in my hand. *It had my wine in it*. He told me I was wearing pink capri pants – although he didn't call them that because he didn't know what capri pants were, he just said pink trousers. He told me I was wearing a white top with a black picture on the front. *My rock 'n' roll t-shirt*. I looked around but couldn't see him. I asked where he was. He said he was watching me, *obviously*. I had meant *where geographically*, which I think he knew. He told me he was working which was the part I'd already figured out. I laughed. He laughed. I still couldn't work out where he was looking from, but he clearly had a good view. *Strange*.

These were the moments when I could never figure him out. Why call? Why tell me you're watching me? Why should I care? Why did *he* care? He had spent such a long time giving me these tiny drip, drip, drips of attention. He would be inside me all night then not be seen with me in public the morning after. He would call me any time of day and night and I would pick up but if he was too busy, he wouldn't even bother to respond to my texts. He'd spent so long telling me what I *'wasn't'* to him that I wasn't sure what I actually *'was'*, yet he needed my loyalty, he needed me to know he was always watching me, that he had eyes everywhere. It was clear that he wanted me, but it was in a different way to how I wanted him. *It both fascinated me and petrified me that we had so much common ground and so little common ground all at the same time.*

I spotted my friends and walked to where they were sat, confused but shamefully happy that he had his eyes on me. I relayed the story about him calling and watching me. One of the girls pointed to where he'd be able to see me from. She'd been in the building before and said it was a clear view. It made sense. I still thought it odd that he would have just been looking out of the window and spotted me in the distance. At the very least it was a coincidence. I wondered if someone had told him my plans.

I drank my cheap, fizzy, and by now lukewarm wine sitting on the grass in the heat feeling my arms getting warm and starting to turn pink. My legs itched from been bitten but the bugs weren't the only thing irritating me. *Why had he called?* I couldn't shake the question. Because someone who didn't give a fuck wouldn't need me to know they were watching me. Surely they would just watch quietly? Someone who did give a fuck might think it's cute to call and say 'I've just spotted you, have a great time'. But this wasn't about whether he gave a fuck or not, this was becoming about me proving myself. He was pushing and pushing. Putting trip hazards in my way. Would I fall, would I stay on my feet? Was I loyal as I said? He was never there but I was always there. He was never present but he wanted me to be omnipresent.

I was free but I wasn't *really* free. I could go out, but someone would be looking for me, watching me, checking my reactions. If another guy paid me any attention did I enjoy it? Did I respond to it? Was I really all about him? Was he truly the only one that I wanted? And at what point would I just say 'fuck this'? It turned out we were closer to that moment than either of us thought.

He had started to call me more now. He called me late one night. We talked about our families. I liked it when he opened up. He told me he was close with his mum. I already knew this because he had called me from his mum's house once when he'd had blisters from his work boots, an occupational hazard, and he told me she was rubbing his feet as we talked. Sweet. I don't know if she knew anything about me but I'm guessing I wasn't as much of a dirty secret as I used to be if he was talking to me at the same time as she was sorting his blisters.

He sometimes asked me about my family. He asked me about the north. Specifically Yorkshire. Southerners seemed incessantly interested in the sayings that we had and still used. Sometimes I felt like people were taking the piss. Especially the 'posher' ones amongst the group. Not Lewis. Some people though. I'm certain they thought I was the stupid northerner with the accent. *Ey' up love it's grim up north int' it.* When I first moved to London I often tried to dial down my accent a little so I didn't stand out as much. *It's something I have never done again.*

I told Lewis that where I'm from the men sometimes refer to the women as 'our lass'. I said sometimes brothers refer to their sisters as 'our lass' or sometimes boyfriends refer to their girlfriends like that. I said my brothers sometimes referenced me like that. He said *'but you're not their lass, you're my lass'*. It made me smile. Really smile. He said it again, *'you're my lass aren't you'*. It wasn't a question. I was his. I would always be his. *Always.*

He asked what I was doing. I said nothing. I was in bed because it was midnight and I'd been talking to him for the last 2 hours. I said he could come around if he wanted to. *Booty call.* He said he would see if he could borrow a car or maybe flag a cab. He arrived 2 hours later. *At 2am It felt like a booty call.*

Something about him was shifting. I couldn't be precise. Just a shift. Maybe a good one but it was hard to tell. We kissed and we undressed and we went to bed. It might sound odd but for once we were totally naked.

There is definitely something more intimate about sex when your bodies are completely bare skin, touching, sweating, sticking. He put my legs up over his shoulders as he entered me and he looked straight in my eyes and asked if I could feel how deep he was. I kissed him. *I'd always been able to feel how deep he was.* I hoped he could feel how deep I was. I think he already knew. I think he ignored that knowledge. Afterwards we laid on the bed and played Marvin Gaye's *'Let's get it on'* as he smoked.

He next called me on a Sunday night. I didn't usually work Sundays in the bar but I did have lectures the next day. It was 9pm. It was raining heavy rain. Torrential. He told me that him and a friend were on their way out to a pub in town and I did I want to come? I couldn't have considered a refusal of any kind but I wasn't ready to go out. I was ready for bed. It was dark and I didn't have much money but this was him asking me properly if I wanted to go out in public. He actually had no objections to been seen with me. He had never done this before.

I rushed to get ready. I wanted to look nice. I wasn't prepared for this. Not. At. All. I pulled on a black dress with black knee-high stiletto boots. My favourite boots. I ran down the communal stairs from my flat and out into the rain trying to work my umbrella and stay upright on the wet pavement. I needed to get the bus to the tube station and then get the tube to where he was. It would take a while. *Shit*. Something happened and my left ankle went over making me trip. My heel had caught in a crack and snapped off 10 yards from the bus stop. *For the love of fucking God*. I had on boots, one without a heel, and a rapidly swelling ankle. If I was a superstitious person I might have thought something was trying to tell me not to go. *But superstitions were for those not in control of their own lives weren't they?*

I ran home as quickly as I could, heel in hand, trying to balance myself out on one good leg and another wobbly one. My hair stuck to my face and my umbrella was doing nothing to protect me against the lashing weather. He called me lots to see where I was. I told him I was still coming. He said to hurry, they were waiting for me. It wouldn't be far off closing time when I reached him. He said they would make their way to the next place and he would text me the details. I ran up the stairs to my 3rd floor flat, rummaged through my wardrobe for anything to put on my feet. Brown boots would do. They hurt but they would do and maybe putting on another pair of boots would keep my ankle from swelling anymore. Worth a shot. I didn't have time to dry off. I needed to get that bus. I re-traced my steps back out into the late Sunday evening and ran until I couldn't run anymore.

When I arrived he said they were going somewhere else that opened late. We got in a black cab and I was grateful for the respite that sitting down and taking the weight off of my fucked up foot gave me. We reached a lowly lit bar where we were the only customers. There was only us three. Me, Lewis and another guy. I knew the guy because he had fucked Izzy a while ago and they'd had a bit of an 'on/off' thing for a few months. I also knew him because he was the one who'd caught us on the black leather couch having sex in a sleeping bag. We laughed about it. It seemed so long ago.

He came back to mine. That had become our thing. He stayed the night saying he would walk to the tube with me in the morning on my way to uni. He'd had on blue jeans, brown boots and a crisp white shirt that he wore with the sleeves rolled halfway up his forearms. In the morning, and without a fresh layer of gel, his hair was slightly floppy at the front and his blue eyes were tinged with pink from lack of sleep or drinking or both. He still made me breathe deeply when I looked at him. My heart pounded every time he walked in a room. That had never gone away. It had never got any less. Having him with me in the morning was weird and wonderful but mostly weird. We'd never *truly* been together in the morning. We'd never walked to a tube station together. Not just the two of us. We walked and talked. My ankle ached from my trip the previous evening, so my walk was more of a hobble though I tried hard disguise it. I didn't want to have to relay the story about getting his text but already being in bed and then having to rush to get ready and then running for the bus and then breaking the heel on my best boots, that I couldn't afford to replace, and then running home to change on an already swelling ankle and then retracing my steps back to the bus stop to get on the tube to get to him. I didn't want to verbalise the lengths I was willing to go to in order to be with him. I didn't want to relay *that* story because I didn't want to be *that* girl.

He was doing that thing again where he kept a safe distance. To outsiders we would look like nothing but acquaintances walking along the street. Maybe colleagues. Maybe a couple who'd been together a long time and had checked out, just going through the motions.

It would have been hard to notice any chemistry between us. If you looked at me closely enough, you could tell by the way I looked at him that I was crazy in love with him. If you looked closely enough at him, you could tell by the way he looked at me that he knew I was crazy in love with him.

He asked me about uni and my lectures, how were they going, what happened once I had my degree. I was reading Law and Mass Communications so the plan was always to go to Law school. Well that was everyone's else plan for me anyway. He thought I was clever. *Was I a swot at school?* Not really. I was the in-between kid. Not part of the cool gang, not part of the nerdy crowd. I hit it somewhere in the middle. Academically able, but not so gifted that I stood out in any of my top set classes. I managed to glide under the radar for most of high school. I guessed he was a cool kid at school. I guessed everyone loved him. I imagined the boys wanted to be him and the girls wanted to go out with him. I thought his charismatic aloofness would attract people to him. I imagined his depth would scare people away. He thought it would be cool to be a lawyer and that I didn't need him around. That I should go and fly. Be a big shot. Little did he know that I wasn't doing so well at getting to be a big shot because my mind had been so absorbed by him that I hadn't really been concentrating on my lectures.

It was the first time I'd heard anything like insecurity from him. I think that's what it was. Like he was saying he wasn't good enough for me. *I was going to have a career. A life. I had to go live it.* He was wrong. We were just over a year apart at birth. We shared the same star sign. *I read them for us daily*. We had shared passions and loves. We were intense people. We felt deeply. We were both capable of cutting too deep. Deep enough to damage. Deep enough to hurt. We fell in and out of things hard and quick. We were obsessed. We were each other's strange obsession. We were never truly together yet rarely apart. He watched me from a distance. I watched him close up. If we carried on down this road it would kill us.

I never did get my ankle checked. *It still makes a clicking sound to this day.*

Tidal Wave

Tidal wave has two meanings. The first is a large ocean wave and the second is 'an overwhelming manifestation of an emotion'. This was my constant state now. I was a torrent of high and low, day after day, night after night. Weeks had turned into months, the months into almost a couple of years. I was in so deep that I couldn't escape. *Did I even want to escape?* My friends were tired of hearing about it. They were tired of my angst. They were tired of the drama. They had dramas of their own. Cheating sagas. Unwanted pregnancies. STI's. Drug issues.

They were tired of my inability to be coherent about anything else other than him. My own being had become so wrapped up in him that I'd lost all sense of myself. Like any addict I needed a regular shot of him otherwise the pain was too excruciating to bear. Like any addict I was withdrawing from real life in favour of my next fix. For me the fix was always the high of been with him. The fantasy of him being mine. The idea that one day it would be reality. Like any addict I had to be enabled. What I couldn't quite decide was who was most guilty of doing the enabling. Him. *Or me?*

The fixes came in small doses. Whenever he could manage it. Whenever he wasn't working. Whenever he wasn't out with the boys. Whenever he'd been listening to music that reminded him of one of our many shared moments of pleasure and pain. *It had all been built on pleasure and pain.*

I can't really recall this part in any detail. I can tell you the basics of what happened. I can tell you the why's. I can explain some of the fall out. I can convey the embarrassment. I can write about the devastation. But it's not quite as clear as everything else. It's in the depths of my mind for very good reason. It was stupid. It hurt. Him. *And me.*

It was coming up to our birthday's. I think we went out for his but he didn't turn up for mine. I don't remember why but I don't think it was because of work because if it had been I would never have done what I did. I suppose that, on top of months of to'ing and fro'ing, he wants me, he doesn't want me, I'm his, I'm not his, had just taken its toll. I always knew we'd implode I just didn't know it'd be me that was responsible.

We were enjoying cocktails and shots. The guys had this weird thing they did with tequila shots where they drank, licked the salt from the back of their hands and then squirted the lemon juice directly into their eye. I'd seen them do it a few times in various bars and was baffled every time. I found it odd at best and fucking ridiculous at worst. What would possess grown men to do that? *Was it the equivalent of a pissing contest?*

I was upset he hadn't turned up. It seemed like a shitty thing to do. I was getting pissed off with being watched by his friends, being out with them but not him, with putting on a brave face, plastering on a smile, and being completely single but having to act like I wasn't. When would it ever end? Did I want it to end? What could I do to make him understand? What I did next would answer that question.

In walked new guy. The one they all thought was a knob. The one who I *might* have had I not had a thing with Lewis. We chatted. We drank. We danced. We kissed. *Everyone saw the kiss.* Lots of the guys Lewis worked with saw. Someone had a camera. Someone took a photo. *Someone took lots of photos*. I believe it to have been Izzy. I figured she was probably lapping this up. There had always been something about the way she reacted to me and Lewis that was just, well, *odd*. Somehow *off.* I had photos taken with the new guy of us laughing and enjoying the night. This was before camera phones. There was no option to delete. Once those photos had been developed the evidence was hard evidence. I looked happy in the photos. I looked like I was having fun in the photos. I *was* having fun in the photos. *Fuck.*

We didn't sleep together. We didn't go home together. But that kiss effectively ended everything I had with Lewis. Of course he quickly found out what I'd done. I'm certain at least a handful of people had taken great glee in making sure he found out as soon as possible. I believe that to have also been Izzy. I heard from everyone we collectively knew that he was pissed off. Really pissed off. He was raging. *That I'd blown it.*

There was some element of trying to reason with him. Text messages that he ignored. Text messages that he responded to. *It didn't mean anything. I was hurt he wasn't there.* It wasn't an excuse. I couldn't condone my behaviour. *It was him I wanted* but what the fuck were we even doing anyway? I wasn't the girlfriend. *I was barely the friend.* Was he really saying he didn't want me but no one else could want me either? Was he just pissed off he'd lost the easiest lay he'd ever had? Was his pride hurt? Male ego? *Why did someone who cared so little suddenly care so much?*

He was completely unreasonable, failing to recall the girlfriend situation he'd had going on for at least several months of us knowing each other. Failing to recall the point he'd made that no longer having a girlfriend meant nothing for 'us'. Failing to recall every time he'd let me down. Failing to recall the distance he had continually put between us. Failing to understand that if he'd have ever shown any actual genuine interest once in all this time, and I don't mean 'I'm watching you in the park' bullshit interest, I'd never have done it. If he'd showed he cared, if he'd not done everything in his power to treat me like something worthless that he could pick up and drop at his whim, then I would never have even looked in anyone else's direction. *I loved him. I adored him. I was obsessed with him.* I couldn't deal with the pain of not having him. He had been everything for so long that I couldn't imagine a day when I wouldn't think about him. *That would be an abiding feeling for many, many years.*

Everyone told me it was worse because of *who* I'd kissed. I got it. They really didn't like each other. It was the worst possible choice of person. *It was the most perfect choice of person.* If you're going to fuck something up, you may as well fuck it up properly. That's exactly what I'd done. *So I'd probably lose nothing else by actually fucking him.*

Me and the new guy, well we fell into an easy kind of 'seeing/shagging/using each other' rhythm. There's an old adage about getting under someone to get over someone else. That's all I was doing. Maybe he knew my heart wasn't really in it, but he only ever mentioned that once when he asked me outright if I was fucking him to get back at Lewis. I told him it was nothing. It meant nothing. It hadn't been anything. Anyway, it was over, who cared? *I cared.* I'd learned to be amazing at faking how I felt. I'd spent a long time pretending I was okay, I was happy, I was detached enough to not care. Now I'd thrown myself into this situation I was doing well at faking falling in some kind of something with someone else.

By now I'd moved flats again, a hazard of both the London rental market, dodgy landlords and the desire to add Izzy to our flat share and try and cut the ridiculous amount we had to hand over each month to pay someone else's mortgage. Also an old adage – *Keep your friends close and your enemies closer*. I had never been sure I could trust her and now my gut instinct was screaming that she was loving this.

We rented a flat in a trendy part of East London in a purpose-built art deco style block complete with a lift, the type that has those double doors you pull across and that you can see through all the way up. The lift and the black and white chequered floor gave the place a more upmarket feel. We'd gone up in the world. We were now in the midst of proper adulting with uni finished, an upgraded post code and a small breakfast bar where we made cherry brandy, amaretto and sour cocktails on Friday evenings before we went out. We poured them neat over crushed ice, revelling in the adultness of taking the alcohol out of the cupboards, precisely pouring the perfect measures of each ingredient and sipping out of whatever glasses were available. It was a nicer place, I was told, than the grotty flat we'd been renting that had seen better days and had only had a rubber handheld attachment on the taps and not an actual shower. This was what new guy had said to me anyway, having been the only man who, to date, had visited both places.

I was now picking up work as a Paralegal in various places across London trying to make ends meet and find the £500 per month for rent that I had committed to as well as bills, food and travel. If I'd had any delusions of following in the glamourous legal footsteps of Ally McBeal they'd been quickly and quietly knocked out of me whilst lugging around legal files that were heavier than one of my own legs, on and off tubes, up and down station stairs, so that the Barrister who was dealing with the case in court didn't have to. And all for the bargain price of £40 per day, which is what the legal aid firm I was currently working for were paying me. If I finished before 2pm it was £20. To this day I have no idea how they got away with it. All I could ask myself was what the fuck had I done going into a career that everyone else were so certain was right for me but that was clearly so wrong. It had long since dawned on me, whilst running up credit card bills, overdrafts and skipping paying bills to buy food, that I'd chosen a life path – or rather had it been chosen for me – that I neither suited nor could afford. I'd paid my own tuition fees, rent and bills out of my student loan, taken any part time jobs I could, worked more hours than a Law student should considering the amount of study I was meant to be doing, and was still struggling. I'd chosen a path that only the middle-class children of the world should choose. Those whose parents paid their fees and their rent and sent them a weekly allowance. I'd had the audacity to rise above my station and now I was falling. *I was a fucking disaster*. There was currently no area of my life that was going well but at least there was equilibrium.

Things had not improved between me and Lewis. We didn't talk, but unfortunately having the same group of friends meant we were in a lot of the same places at the same time. We desperately tried to avoid each other at all costs, but I could quite often feel his eyes boring into me across a room. It was as palpably awkward as it sounds and worse when I was with new guy too. I got the feeling they couldn't have hated each other any more if they tried. I spent most of the time in a state of permanent mortification, plastering on a smile but dying inside. The tension made it difficult to breathe. That, and Lewis's presence anywhere. I still loved him. I still wanted him. I missed him. I hated myself. There was no one I wanted more than him. There was no one I thought about more than him. *But he hated me.*

If we were out as a group, I watched him laughing, dancing, drinking and looking like he was happy. Maybe he was happy. He'd successfully got me out of his life, well his personal life anyway, and there's a good chance he was relieved, not mourning the loss of me at all. He tried to never make eye contact with me because he knew as well as I did that would be dangerous. I never saw him flirt with or kiss another girl and for that I was eternally grateful. I was desperate never to hear on the grapevine that he was seeing someone else. I internally prayed that no one would ever have to tell me that. For their sake and mine. It may have been just coincidence, I had no real idea of what, or who, he was doing, but if he did it out of any type of respect, I appreciated the sentiment.

When I went to Scotland for a night for new guy's first 'Family Day' it was very weird to be in the same place, in the same pub, although thankfully not in the same room, and a relief that I wasn't going to the actual day itself – that was kept for his mum and his young son who he'd fathered with his ex-girlfriend before he joined the army.

New guy had kept me waiting for hours that night. He was notoriously unreliable. I called and called to say I'd arrived, sitting in the pub alone feeling conspicuous and stupid. *Why had I come here? What was I doing?* I knew that he was fucking other women regularly, a fact I chose not to acknowledge but that everyone had warned me. Still, I clung to the idea of making this one the one that stuck. Maybe it was ironic that old guy and new guy hated each other yet were guilty of the exact same behaviour. Maybe this was what it was like to wear the shoe on the other foot. *Maybe I deserved it?*

When he finally showed up hours later, making some excuse about his car I guessed that he'd been getting rid of the evidence of another woman – they met lots on exercise in Scotland for weeks' every summer – and maybe it had taken him that long to make his excuses to her, while keeping me waiting. It was feasible. But strangely it was him that gave me some sense of normality. It was him who I went to Tesco's shopping with and it was him that I ate with and it was him that slept in bed next to me all night, not leaving before sunrise so he wouldn't be seen. He also always kissed me in public. Always held my hand. He was a player. A bad boy. A bit of a cad. But he was very fucking good at it.

Someone would later tell me that I'd called it right and that he'd been sleeping with someone else. It was not a surprise. I already knew. *Always trust your gut instinct.*

We kept going with this dance for a while. It all ended when after not being able to get hold of him for hours, and something telling me I was about to get my just desserts, a female voice picked up his phone. He was in the shower, she heard his phone going and picked up. After some weird introductions that entailed stating the town we lived in, how long we'd known him and if we were sleeping with him – the answers to which for both of us were London, a few months and yes, we realised that we were both the 'other woman'. I felt sorrier for her than for me simply because I'd known, or at least suspected, and was slightly more prepared than she clearly was. *She had not suspected.* Not only that, but I'd been warned. By his colleagues, by my friends and by the man I was still, and always had been, in love with. *Oh, and she told me she was pregnant.*

The Wedding

The wedding of mutual friends was approaching. It was a Register Office affair, with only a few people invited to the ceremony and a bigger reception afterwards. The hen and stag was a joint night out, with the girls starting in a restaurant for dinner, the guys going elsewhere and then all meeting in a bar in Leicester Square. I didn't go to the meal on account of the restaurant being too expensive. I knew I wouldn't be able to afford my part of the bill and then go on drinking, so I chose to only do the latter, making up some excuse about work and not getting there on time.

The joint aspect of the night might have been awkward because colleagues of the husband to be would be there and that would include Lewis. Strangely, and as I only found out when the guys arrived, neither Lewis nor the new guy were there. Apparently both were working. I wondered if they were working together. *Wouldn't that be ironic*. I wondered how they felt about that. Whether they were civil. Whether they conversed about our situation.

New guy - No, it wasn't anything, neither of us were that into it.

Lewis - That's because she's in love with me.

New guy - If she was in love with you why did she sleep with me?.

Lewis - To get back at me. To hurt me.

New guy - If you were bothered about her you'd still be with her. You'd make the effort to be with her. It's only your pride that's hurt.

Lewis - Maybe.

The wedding was worse. Much worse. And would end in yet more tears. *My tears.*

The Register Office was impressive with beautiful grey stone stairs leading up to the main doors. It was a busy London day and people stopped outside to look at the guests, hoping to catch a glimpse of the bride. I'd be lying if I said I hadn't imagined getting married to Lewis. What it would be like if all these people were here for us. What it would be like to stand and look him in the eye and tell him I was his. *Always. Forever.*

The Ceremony was sweet and quick and being a few rows back on the bride's side meant I could see the back of most of the groom's side heads. *He wasn't there.* He was working. Another occupational hazard. Not all men could ever be at personal events together, even weddings.

I could see the back of new guy's head. He'd said he might not be able to make it a few weeks ago, but apparently here he was. We didn't make eye contact once. I didn't particularly care. It wasn't that deep anymore. It never had been in the first place even though I'd lied to myself and everyone else that it was. He had never been the one I imagined being stood up there with, all the eyes on us, saying 'I do'. I couldn't have given a shit whether he was there or not there, we held no animosity towards each other and we could definitely be civil at a wedding.

Someone told me to expect Lewis at the reception. *At least they'd given me fair warning.* Apparently he was finishing work and could make the evening part. I was glad I'd really dressed up. Wedding sexy. I was wearing cream and gold wide leg trousers, a gold top and gold heels and I'd styled my shoulder length hair in loose curls. I thought my arse looked good in the trousers. I'd lost some weight. The heartbreak diet they call it. But I still worked out so I was the epitome of pert and firm. It was easy to spot him when I walked in. He was already at the bar.

The room was just big enough for us to avoid each other had he moved from the bar at all. Unfortunately, and maybe on purpose, he decided that's where he would spend all evening. I did everything in my power to get friends to go to the bar, for one of the guys to take my card and grab me a drink. Anything to stay as physically far away as possible. But as people got more drunk, they were much less inclined to be kind or even bothered about whether me and Lewis could stand next to each other without ripping off each other's heads or each other's clothes. No-one, even us, was ever quite sure which it might be and everyone we knew was over it. We were either together or not together. Sort it out. Or don't. But it was clear no one wanted to end up as collateral damage in the middle of our shit anymore.

Standing right next to him at the bar meant I had to order really quickly. Having his eyes burning holes into my back made it impossible to concentrate and I couldn't even process the liquid options. My friend was drinking Campari and lemonade, so I ordered the same. The sooner I could escape from the bar and being stood within touching distance of Lewis the better. I made a mental note to myself that Campari is fucking disgusting. I feel the same about Aperol now. But there was no way I was going back to that bar, I'd rather die of thirst. Or sobriety.

I did everything I could to make light of it. I danced with the girls and I chatted to the guys. I looked over at him almost constantly the way you do when there is something you know you shouldn't stare at but you have no bodily control over where your eye line lands. He was quite often looking back. He still hated me I could tell because this wasn't the looking across the room watching me broodingly, this was glaring at me hoping I'd disappear. He wasn't alone in wanting that. I spent all night wanting the ground to swallow me up too.

When the first dance came it was awkward. The happy couple wanted everyone to join in towards the end. Grab your partners. But I was there alone. And my friends had their respective other halves/part time shags there with them. I was happily going to make myself scarce when someone took my arm and said 'let's dance'. Tall, dark and handsome. It was a guy called Kelvin. I'd known him the entire time I'd known Lewis and we got on well. Had there been no Lewis there might have been potential with him because we definitely had a flirty vibe – a rapport - but mostly we were just mates, and he was doing what a mate would do. He was saving my fucking arse. I've never been more grateful for someone swooping in and acting like a knight in shining armour. I'll never forget how kind he was to me that evening.

He was a close friend of Lewis and he knew that Lewis wasn't speaking to me. He also knew just how crazy in love I was with him. We'd had some conversations over the past couple of years where we'd talked about relationships, the girls he was into, the guy I was into. We talked at least once about his previous experiences with Izzy, who had slept with him and then binned him for one of the other guy's he worked with and who was a higher rank. I got the impression she'd hurt him and that he'd been into her. That he thought it could've gone somewhere. He understood a bit of what I felt about Lewis because he'd had a little taste of it with Izzy.

When everyone started to couple up on the dancefloor, he saw me head for the hills and he didn't want me to run. In the forces you styled it out. You faced up to it. He said I had no reason to run, that I was meant to be here as much as anyone else, I'd been invited, I had every right to be here and enjoy it. In the army you did whatever the fuck you could to save your arse or the arse of someone else who needed saving. That night I needed saving.

We slow danced and chatted. They danced their first married dance to 'Crazy for You' by Madonna. I don't know if they could've chosen a more appropriate song. *'I see you through the smoky air …… you're so close but still a world away ….. I never wanted anyone like this ….. I'm crazy for you'*. I'm certain Lewis would not have liked the choice of song. I'm certain he would have referred to it as utter shite. That it made him want to vomit listening to it. I'm certain he'd have chosen something deeper. More meaningful. He would have discounted this as shallow, too simple, pop. But as I listened to those words there weren't any lyrics that would have said what I was feeling more accurately. All he needed to do was listen. All he needed to do was feel. All he needed to do was understand. *I didn't know how I could get him to do any of those things.*

Kelvin told me not to take any of it to heart. That everyone would get over it. That Lewis would get over it. That he'd come around. That he's not the type to hold a grudge. And the new guy, how did I feel about that? *I felt nothing about it, it wasn't really anything anyway.* Kelvin saved me from feeling like an idiot that night. I would've been alone. The only one in the room with no one to dance with. The only one in the room with someone who truly hated them. He saved me from collapsing into a heap and ruining someone's wedding. It was a surprise when he took me by the hand and led me outside and kissed me. *It was even more of a surprise when I kissed him back.*

He was just playing. He didn't mean any harm. It was just flirting. It was just a kiss. It was just a moment in time. I was neither offended nor bowled over. He never meant it to lead anywhere, and it didn't. That night he was just kind enough to give me some company, to make me feel less like shit than I already did. It compounded what I already thought about him – he was a nice guy. One of the good ones. Despite being really good looking and confident, the type you would think was an absolute dick, he'd proved himself to be nothing but a gent, willing to sweep in and pick up the pieces of something that was nothing to do with him, and that he really didn't need to get involved in. Something he would likely feel some heat from back at the barracks. Why did you dance with her? Why did you take her outside? Why are you on her side? Why the fuck didn't you just leave it alone?

We never kissed or talked about the kiss again afterwards, and he never put any pressure on me to take it any further either on the night or afterwards. If anything, we just became better friends and I realised that some men were just good people through and through. It just always turned out to be the ones you didn't expect.

En Español

It was almost his birthday. I wouldn't be able to top my first birthday gift to him of the CD, but I needed it to be just as personal. We had talked about what he would do after the army. He told me he wanted to leave. That they broke you down as a person so they could build you back up again into what they wanted you to be. He didn't like it. He hadn't wanted to be broken into someone else. He wanted to be him. The army had just been a stop gap, not a long term thing. He said he'd dreamed of moving abroad somewhere warm – He liked Spain. I told him I'd done a summer season in Spain before uni and that I was trying to learn Spanish. That I was getting okay at it. That it was a nice language and a nice country.

My summer had been spent working in a busy cabaret bar as a table waitress, eventually graduating to cocktail bar tender towards the end of the season. Much to my parents dismay I'd bought a one-way flight on the promise of a job but with nowhere to live. I definitely had an adventurer inside me. *Either that or I was incredibly good at running away*. When I turned up to the bar to take up the job offer, I happened upon a girl about my age who already worked there and offered me the sofa in her 11th floor apartment. The Copacabana had no working lift, cockroaches and balconies that were questionable on safety standards, but it felt exotic and grown up and I had a very hot and sweaty summer sleeping on a threadbare sofa bed in an apartment that didn't have a fan let alone air conditioning. I spent 3 months listening to The Corrs on repeat, sunbathing topless for the first time, practising my novice Spanish on kind but clearly bored taxi drivers and trying to find a working payphone to reverse charge call my mum weekly to tell her I was still alive. It was neither my best nor worst move, but I learned a lot about life that summer – I have 14 takeaways I can share:

1. Men lie.
2. So do women.
3. I know when someone is lying.
4. I can lie when I need to.
5. Communication is hard when you don't speak the same language.
6. People use drugs more than you think.

7. Pizza Hut tastes different there than it does here.
8. So does Diet Coke.
9. Danger is everywhere.
10. So is obsession.
11. People hurt me often.
12. I allowed people to hurt me. Often.
13. If you live by the adage 'suspect everyone and trust no one' you'll do well.
14. If you live by the adage 'suspect everyone and trust no one' you might not do well.

When you spoke Spanish it sounded loaded with sex. It was a language that made you feel as though you'd just arrived in a hot country. That feeling when you step off the plane and the heat hits all your senses at once and then you can smell the air and it smells so different to the air at home and if you stand still enough you can feel it seeping into your skin. I could imagine Lewis speaking it to me. *Te amo para siempre.*

No. The army was never for him. He wanted a simple, fuss free life. I could definitely see him as nomadic. A wanderer, roaming around wherever life took him, guitar over his shoulder, cigarettes in his pocket and a dog or two following. I think it suited him. I wished it suited me but that's not what life had mapped out for me.

I thought of the perfect gift. When I was a kid people always brought back lighters from their holidays. It reminded them of their perfect place. Their perfect memories. Every time they lit a cigarette it would be there. That flame. At first a flicker then something bigger. If you held your thumb down the flame was constant, only going out when you let go. *The trick was to never let go.* Then it was safely tucked away in their pocket for safe keeping. How could you get any closer to a body than a lighter in a pocket? I found a heavy chrome lighter and took it to the local locksmiths. It wasn't cheap but nothing worthwhile came cheap or easy. I was having it engraved with his initials and one simple word. *Siempre.* It means '*always*' in Spanish. It seemed like a nice touch. A nod to the future. A nod to the past. Maybe he would go live in Spain. Maybe I would too. And maybe this had all gone too far.

I had it boxed and then put it in a brown padded envelope and wrote his name on it. I asked Izzy to pass it onto him through the guy she was sleeping with who still had a girlfriend and who still wore his crucifix.

We had managed by this point to be civil to each other. In fact, he was softening towards me. He didn't hate me anymore, we were something that resembled the weirdest of friends. We ticked along in social situations but the stares weren't hateful anymore, they were simply the stares of two people who longed to go back to the way it was before. To go back to what we'd had. What we'd experienced with each other. Except I had no desire to go back to the way it had been. I looked at him in the way I'd always looked at him because I still loved him. *Because I would never not love him*. There was never a question in my mind that I would ever be able to stop looking at him the way I did. *It just wasn't an option.*

At some point we talked. Properly talked. But it was on his terms and not mine. Had it meant anything with the new guy? *No*. Why did I do it?

I'm not sure. But I know it's because you missed my birthday. And didn't answer my texts. And ignored me in public. And called me when it suited you. And never showed you cared. And gave me everything and nothing at the same time. And made me hate myself. And made me hate my life. And made me question myself. And because you knew that I loved you and took advantage of it. And you knew that I hung on your every word. And you knew you were leading me on. And you knew you had my heart. And my soul. And you shared things with me and then made those things feel insignificant. I know it's because of those things. And I know it's really because You. Just. Didn't. Fucking. Love. Me.

Those were the things that I *wanted* to say. In reality I said none of those things.

I have no idea how we ended up sleeping together again but we did. He told me he was going to Majorca with his friends. Maybe he'd see what it was like to get a job out there. How much it cost to live there. Maybe he could do it after he left the army. I thought it was a good idea although the thought of him on a boy's holiday filled me with dread. He was single, good looking and he wore a uniform for a living – he was literally a living, breathing magnet for women.

He went on holiday and didn't contact me the entire time. I wasn't surprised because we were definitely not in the place we were before but it didn't stop me fretting. It didn't stop the constant thoughts. The constant worry. Still, we'd made progress. Baby steps but still steps.

He sent me a message when he got back. I asked how it was and he replied 'it was okay'. I was grateful for the lack of detail and the lack of enthusiasm. I hoped he was telling me the truth. I hoped it was just okay. I hoped he had every reason not to be enthusiastic about his holiday.

About a week later he came around to my flat. It was the middle of the day. I couldn't recall the last time I'd seen him, if ever, in the afternoon. We made small talk about his holiday, about work. I wanted to ask him outright if he'd slept with anyone while he was in Majorca. I didn't ask him, but I would soon get the answer.

We had sex that afternoon, on my bed, half clothed, for no reason. It was the most detached sex I'd ever had. Missionary. Flat. Boring. Pointless. Devoid of any rhythm. Not even looking at each other. Painfully sad.

I think we both knew that day that it was over. I think we knew it was goodbye. I think we both realised afterwards that it was an awful way to end something that had, for a long time been filled with passion and music and experience and heat and sex. *The messy intensity that came with unbelievable attraction and incomprehensible connection.* It would have been better to leave well alone. It might have been better to have carried hating each other from across crowded rooms.

Someone would tell me a few days later that he'd met someone on holiday. I've no idea who that someone was or whether it lasted, but I packed my stuff and without saying a word to anyone I walked away from London. I would be back, but not until after my big military wedding.

I've no idea if he ever received the lighter for his birthday, but if he did he never mentioned it to me.

The beginning of the end

8 years later I finally filed for divorce. From the man I married that was not Lewis. From the man I married to try to replace *Lewis*. Who I'd met on a girls holiday and got into a weird 'rebound' relationship with. I moved out of the marital home and into a small, actually *tiny*, place on the border of London. It crossed my mind that I was not a million geographical miles from Lewis as he was now living back in London too.

He was also separated. Or maybe divorced. Either way they weren't together anymore. *How serendipitous.* Months of social media stalking meant I knew this for a fact. The joys of technology advancement.

A group of us decided to go to the Tattoo convention. On account of the fact I wasn't tattooed it's not my natural stomping ground. The convention will change that. I'm here to have a needle leave an indelible mark on my body.

We have walked around for an hour. There is a vegan cake stall selling cupcakes of varying flavours. I buy a jaffa cake flavour cake. I figure it will serve two purposes – lining my stomach and raising my blood sugar. This is the lady's first time holding a stall here. She tells us it's going well and she's taking orders for birthday cakes. I'm inconveniently vegan so I take a card. There are 3 bars and all of them are busy, several people deep waiting to be served. They serve only drinks in plastic cups although the people here don't strike me as fighters who might use the receptacles as weapons.

It's a sunny day and we go sit on the pavement outside. The cobbled area is busy with people eating, drinking, chatting. A group of guys ask if they can join us. *Why not*. They're all tattooed to various extents, and some have piercings. Not my normal crowd but today is a day to be open to possibilities. They smoke roll ups. I'm not into it. I've only ever kissed one smoker and that was Lewis. On him it was 1950's sexy, on anyone else it seems to serve no purpose.

They say don't drink before having a tattoo because it thins the blood and can cause more bleeding. I've had 3 large gins and not much tonic. The convention is bustling with the heavily tattooed, the punks, the rockers and the uninitiated, un-inked, bare skinned people who are seeking a new obsession. Or maybe they are re-igniting an old one. It is also a place where today, *He* is. I spotted him straight away. It was still so easy for me to sense him in a room.

Serendipity.

Ordinarily I would never trust myself in a room alone with this man but in a room full of people, people with beautiful colours radiating from their bodies depicting love, hate, peace, hope, happiness, even the souls of those already passed, in this room I was safe.

There are tattoo artists from all over the world here. Ami James has drawn a big crowd, maybe because of his talent and maybe because of his television fame stemming from 'Miami Ink'. I am seeking out a particular artist who has travelled from Madrid. I tell him what I want and ask how much it will be to be tattooed on my wrist and he tells me £70. I sit down, lightheaded and flushed from the gin but giddy with excitement at my own bravery that I'm about to let a man I don't know mark me for eternity. *Not for the first time.* I give him my right arm and he cleans the inside of my wrist with an alcohol wipe. The tattoo will be in black ink in cursive lettering. The needle buzzes into action and he dips it into an ink pot. Holding my arm against the table the needle makes contact with my skin. It doesn't hurt, then it hurts, then it scratches, then it bleeds, and he wipes away the blood, then he goes over it another two times and each time the ink goes deeper. Now it hurts like a motherfucker. It takes no longer than 20 minutes. He spreads a thick layer of Vaseline on my wrist and wraps it in cling film. All done. He tells me to keep it clean and don't pick it. *Apparently scabs don't heal if you pick at them.*

The adrenaline is cursing through my veins and everything is pumping hard. I feel like I might faint. Not from pain. Just from the rush. The rush of doing something new, the rush of the crowds, the rush of the alcohol, the rush of the blood, the rush of seeing him *in the flesh* for the first time in 8 years.

Earlier he had walked past me with his group of friends. Twice. His best friend was there. Neither saw me. His presence lingered long after he'd gone. I wondered why he hadn't noticed mine. It crossed my mind that I could use serendipitous reasoning to approach him. The conversation would come easily. We would fall back into our stride, whatever that was.

I can't *believe* it. What a *surprise*. What a *shock*.

How weird that we would both be *here* on the same day.

Me? I just had a tattoo done

How have you been? How's your *wife?*

My *husband?* Oh, that didn't work out. I've filed for divorce.

Because of you.

It was the last time I saw him in person. The non-conversation played out in my mind with various endings. I never did get to tell him about the tattoo on my wrist.

It read '*Siempre*'.

Afterword

All writers draw upon their own life experiences when writing stories of any kind. Contained within these pages you might be tempted that what is written is not fiction but truth. Yet truth can never be definitive. The only truth you can ever hold is your own. Everyone else's differs along with their perspective. So, whilst I drew heavily on my own experiences as a young woman living in London when I was writing this book, those experiences have been moved, changed, switched, altered and fictionalised in a way that the passage of time and the fading of memories is able to achieve.

For every experience I had, and that I used as a basis for the stories in this book, I am truly thankful. That I have lived this life encompassed in such richness, such depth of feeling and such utter fun and that I get to turn them into something which is entertaining, enlightening or enriching for others to read, is incredible.

And in amongst the fictional, the elements that will always remain true are the power of music, friendship, love and life.

Acknowledgements

There are many who inspired or helped me in writing this book. Those who I met back in the day when I first moved to London, particularly the misfits like me who never realised they were great but were some of the greatest people you could know. The man who I loved almost uncontrollably and who introduced me to some pretty cool music. To all and any of my academic supervisors who have critiqued my work and given me the confidence to get the words on the paper. And to anyone else who has ever told me to stop procrastinating and just write. My high school English teacher who inspired my incessant need to draft and re-draft. My husband for putting up with the never-ending stream of self-doubt, imposter syndrome and over-thinking. And for his unwavering support in me writing this book, and the others still to come. And finally, to my baby boys who give me a reason to be better every day. I am immensely proud of you both.

An ode to the music …

Addictive (2002), Truth Hurts. ft Rakim; Aftermath Entertainment/Interscope Records; writers Stephen Garrett, David Blake, William Griffin, Bappi Lahiri

Be Faithful (1999), Fatman Scoop; AV8; writers Freeman, Bini, Rizzo, Combs, Crawford, Emery, Edwards, Evans, Lawrence, Rogers, Alexander, Cauley, Hammond, Jones, McClean, Titus

Crazy for you (1985), Madonna; Geffen/Columbia Records; writers John Bettis, Jon Lind

Cry to Me (1962), Solomon Burke; Atlantic Records; writer Bert Russell, aka 'Bert Berns'

Dilemma (2002), Nelly ft. Kelly Rowalnd; Universal/Columbia Records; writers Nelly, Antoine 'Bam' Macon, Ryan Bowser, Kenneth Gamble, Bunny Sigler

Don't think I'm not (2000), Kandi Burruss; Columbia Records; writers Kandi Burruss, Kevin 'She'kspere' Briggs, Bernard Edwards Jr

End of the road (1992), Boyz II Men; LaFace/Arista/Motown Records; writers Kenneth 'Babyface' Edmonds, Antonio 'L.A' Reid, Daryl Simmons

Green Onions (1962), Booker T and the MGs; Stax Records; writers Booker T. Jones, Steve Cropper, Lewie Steinberg, Al Jackson Jr

How can you mend a broken heart (1972), Al Green; Polydor/ATCO records; writers Barry Gibb, Robin Gibb

If you don't know me by now (1972), Harold Melvin and The Blue Notes; Philadelphia International Records; writers Gamble/Huff

I'll make love to you (1994), Boyz II Men; Motown Records; writer Kenneth 'Babyface' Edmonds

In the Still of the Night (1956), The Five Satins; Standord/Ember Records; writer Fred Parris

Let me blow ya mind (2001), Eve ft Gwen Stefani; Ruff Ryders Entertainment, Interscope Records; writers Jeffers, Young, Elizondo, Storch, Jordan

Let's stay together (1971), Al Green; Hi Records; writers Al Green, Willie Mitchell, Al Jackson Jr

Love Man (1969), Otis Redding; ATCO Records

Me and Mrs Jones (1972), Billy Paul; Philadelphia International; writers Kenny Gamble, Leon Huff, Cary Gilbert

Mercy Mercy Me (1971), Marvin Gaye; Tamla/Motown Records

One sweet day (1995), Mariah Carey and Boyz II Men; Columbia Records; writers Mariah Carey, Walter Afanasieff, Nathan Morris, Michael McCary, Shawn Stockman, Wanya Morris

Rock your body (2003), Justin Timberlake; Jive Records; writers Justin Timberlake, Chad Hugo, Pharrell Williams

Sittin' on The Dock of The Bay (1968), Otis Redding; Stax Records; writers Steve Cropper, Otis Redding

So hard to say goodbye to yesterday (1991), Boyz II Men; Motown Records; a cover of original record by G.C. Cameron released 1975; writers Freddie Perren, Christine Yarian

Some kind of Wonderful (1961), The Drifters; Atlantic Records; writers Gerry Goffin, Carole King

These Arms of Mine (1962), Otis Redding; Stax/Volt Records

Water runs dry (1995), Boyz II Men; Motown Records; writer Kenneth 'Babyface' Edmonds

Printed in Great Britain
by Amazon

86863185R00098